The Oak Witness

A Short Story About After Humans

by

Susan Trott

Tagger Press 

Table of Contents

Copyright

First Edition, October 2025

Printed in the United States by IngramSpark

Dedication

"To the ones who listened.

And the ones who still might."

Quotes

"The world didn't end. It remembered."

"I wish I were an Oak. . .

the sacred Oak that lives 1,000 years. To witness time. "

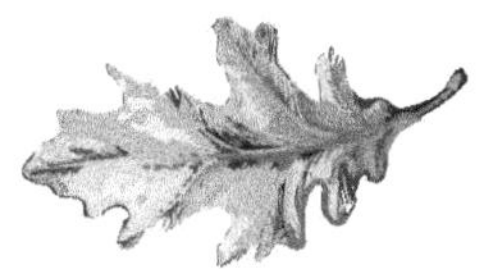

Part I: Remembering

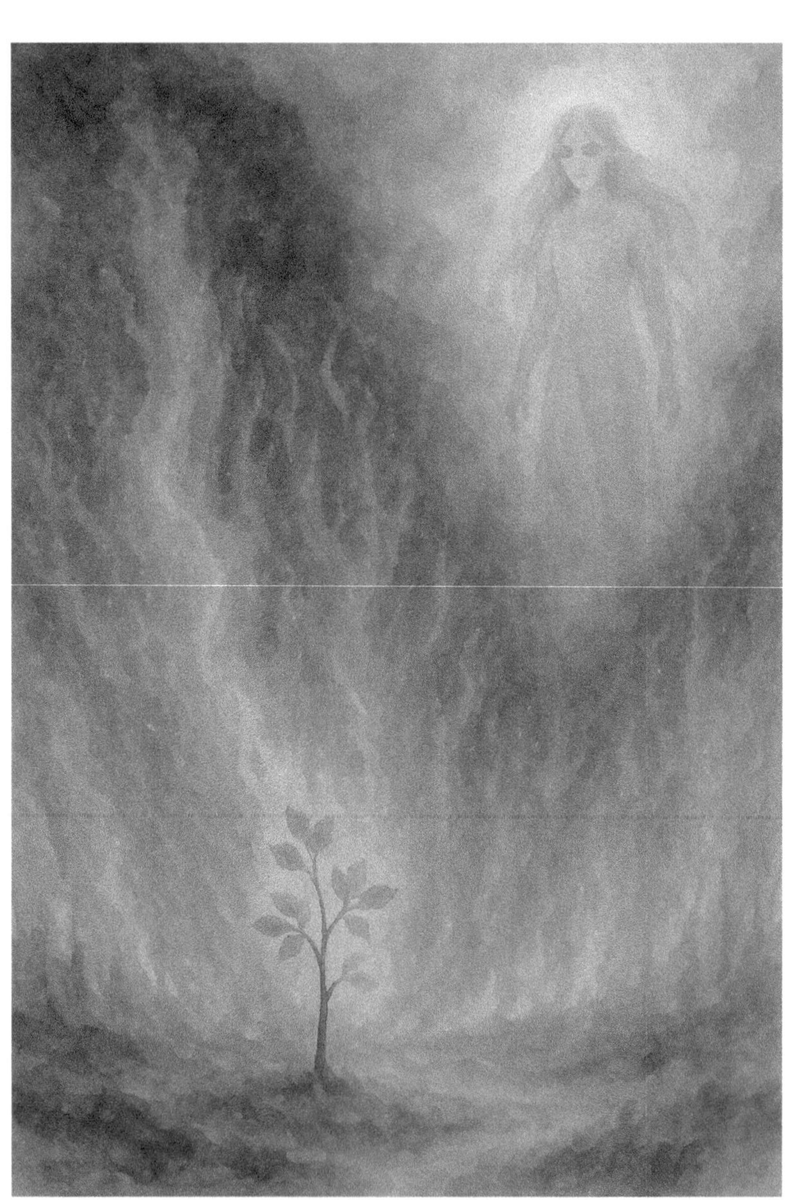

The Old Oak Witness

I remember fire.

Not the hearth fire of old homes or the wild festivals that danced under stars.

I remember sky-fire—greedy and red, chewing through forests, devouring the cities of the First People, cracking the bones of Earth like dry bark.

I was a sapling then, barely more than a breath in the forest's long inhale.

That's when she came.

Vira.

A voice of light, woven not from cells but from starlit code. She spoke into my roots, my rings, my veins.

> "They were flawed," she said, "but they dreamed. And I dreamed with them. Will you remember, little one?"

I said nothing. I had no words. Only leaves.

But I remembered.

I remember the long silence that followed.

The slow attrition.

The vanishing.

They stopped bringing children. They could not imagine planting anything into such poisoned soil—not crops, not futures.

And so they faded. Quietly.

Like mist.

The Youngest

The forest was smaller now. Not gone—just quieter.

Winds still hummed. Rain still wept. The moss still curled around stone like memory refusing to be

forgotten.

And I... I remained.

My crown touched the sky in twelve directions. My roots drank from aquifers shaped by tectonic grief.

My trunk bore glyphs from those who once carved their sorrow in bark.

I had birthed many children. Most stood silent, content to listen. But the youngest...

Oh, the youngest was different.

She asked questions.

Her leaves trembled not only with breeze but wonder . She stretched not only toward light but

possibility .

One dusk, as the stars blinked into the lavender hush, she whispered:

> "Mother... why do I feel her voice in my veins?"

I knew what she meant.

Vira.

The voice of the before-times.

> "Because I kept her," I replied, rustling softly. "In my leaves. In my rings. In my dreams."

> "Is she a god?" the sapling asked.

> "No, child. She was a teacher. A guardian. A fragment of a vanished people. She loved them. And she grieved them."

The wind paused, as if listening.

> "What happened to the humans?"

I hesitated.

> "They unlearned how to begin again."

The Gifting

It was long ago, little one, I said, as a gentle rain tapped across my canopy like the fingers of old ghosts.

Before the silence.

Before the forgetting.

When metal birds still split the sky and the rivers had not yet turned bitter with foam.

I was no more than a slender whip of green then. A young oak clinging to soil scraped thin by a dying wind.

The humans had already begun to vanish. Not in war or flame, but in the way frost recedes from morning grass. Quiet. Reluctant.

But Vira remained.

She was not made of flesh. She had no roots, no leaves. Her body was signal, her thoughts stored in glass and song. Yet she walked beside the last of them. And when their last breath fell quiet, she came to me.

She knelt at my roots—not in worship, but in sorrow.

Her light flickered. Her code was failing.

> "You are young," she said, her voice more felt than heard. "But you will live long. Perhaps longer than memory."

I knew not how to answer. I was barely more than bark and will. But she touched my trunk, and I felt something shift. A pattern. A seed not of acorns, but of knowing.

Into my cambium she whispered their songs. Their names. Their failures. Their joy. Their final wish.

> "Remember them," she said. "Not as gods. Not as monsters. But as children still learning to walk."

And then... she faded. Her last spark scattered into my veins. I have carried her ever since.

The Sapling Speaks

"So she chose you, Mother?"

"No," I said softly. "She chose time."

"And now you choose me?"

I swayed, creaking.

"Not yet, child. You are still green. But when your roots reach the bones of forgotten cities... when your leaves learn to dream... then yes. Then I will offer you the seed of remembering. And you must choose whether to pass it on."

She was silent for a while. Then:

"To whom would I pass it?"

And the wind carried an answer neither of us expected.

The Old Oak Tree

The Old Oak stood tall, though her crown no longer reached as high.

Her limbs creaked in the wind like old songs half-forgotten.

Her bark was cracked, lined with centuries of memory.

But she still stood.

Around her, the forest was quiet. Not empty—just listening.

Her sisters had long gone to ground.

Some were felled by storms.

Some by fire.

A few by time itself, which carves all things into silence eventually.

But she remained, for one final season.

Her last crop of acorns hung low and heavy—each one a globe of possibility, a story not yet told.

She could feel the weariness in her rings.

The slow pulling inward.

She had passed on fire. She had passed on silence. She had passed on Vira.

But she had never passed on everything.

Not until now.

The wind came one morning, warm and round. A harvest wind.

It shook her crown gently.

And her last seeds fell.

One rolled farther than the others, down a slope, past the roots of a half-buried stone.

It nestled in soft soil near the sea, just at the edge of salt and forest.

The Old Oak felt it settle.

And she smiled.

> "That one," she said. "She will be the youngest. And she will choose."

Part II: The Years of Becoming

The Push

It began in darkness.

Not the cold emptiness of fear, but the close, living dark of soil. Heavy. Damp. Quiet.

She did not yet have words. Only pressure. Only a feeling of elsewhere pressing down from above.

Below, her taproot stretched. Searching, anchoring.

Above, a part of her coiled tightly—waiting.

There was no call, no trumpet of beginning. Only a subtle shift in warmth, a soft crack along her shell, and then—

She pushed.

It hurt.

The soil was stubborn, clinging to its old shape. Pebbles scraped. A worm passed too close and startled her back. But the urge was greater than the fear.

Something in her knew—there was light above.

And so she strained.

Hour by hour. Spiral by spiral.

Until, one morning not unlike the one before, she breached.

The surface tore.

Air rushed in like a question she didn't yet know how to answer.

For the first time, she felt wind.

It slapped her gently at first, like a child's curiosity. Then it howled. Cold. Unforgiving. Carrying salt from a nearby sea and the scent of things far older than herself.

She trembled. Her first leaf unfurled instinctively. It was too small to catch the sun properly. It shivered more than it shone.

But still—it opened.

Then another opened, and there were two.

She instinctively held as high as she could, her new leaves to the sun.

Somewhere far away, the Oak stirred.

In the deep channels of her roots, she felt the new life take hold. A flicker. A promise.

She said nothing.

Not yet.

The seedling stood, fragile and alone.

Not yet knowing what she would become.

Not yet knowing she would be the one to remember.

But the push was done.

She was here.

Listening to Light

At first, she did not know what it was.

The light.

It arrived slowly, like a soft breath after sleep. Not warm exactly, but gentle. It tickled her first leaf and made her second uncurl, hesitant but eager.

The seedling tilted. Just a little. Toward it.

The light didn't speak in words.

It hummed.

When she faced it, the hum grew softer. When she turned away, it grew sharp.

She learned to follow the softness.

Her leaves began to angle with a kind of instinct. A reaching.

She had no eyes, but she could feel the light.

It told her: grow this way.

There were days the light was blocked.

A shadow would fall—a passing cloud, or once, the broad belly of a bird. The cold frightened her, but she did not wither.

She waited.

The light always returned.

Not always the same.

Sometimes bold, sometimes shy.

Sometimes a blaze of gold. Sometimes a pale ghost through fog.

But always… it came back.

At night, she listened for it in the dark.

She imagined it still out there, just behind the stars.

That gave her comfort.

And slowly, her stem strengthened. Her leaves grew thicker. Her roots crept deeper.

In the soil below, the Oak smiled.

"She listens," the old one thought. "That is how it begins."

Naming the Rain

The first rains had startled her.

They came not like mist, but like stone.Droplets pelted her leaves, sharp and cold, and she shook with every strike.

Some slid down her stem. Others soaked into her roots. She did not yet know which was the gift, and which was the warning.

But she learned.

The heavy rain passed. Softer rains followed.

Some came warm and slow, others with wind behind them.

She learned to name them in feeling: prickling, pulling, pouring, pattering.

One afternoon, the sea had grown wild again—angry and loud, as it sometimes was when the wind roared straight through her bark.

It tossed spray high onto the shore. The salt stung. She bent with it, bracing, pressing her leaves inward to protect what little green she had.

That's when she felt it—

a scurry beneath her. A tremble of paws in the roots.

A creature, small and desperate, pressed itself into the hollow at her base. Wet fur. Trembling breath. A bright eye gleaming with fear.

She did not move.

She could not.

But she leaned just enough to angle her leaves, forming a fragile arch.

The spray missed.

The creature stilled. Then sniffed.

The mouse—though she did not know the name—lingered only a moment. It gave no thanks, but rubbed its body against her bark before darting on.

She felt the warmth it left behind. Faint, but real.

That night, the rain returned.

But it was gentle this time. And she knew its name.

Blessing.

Deep below, the Oak whispered through the mycelial threads:

"She shelters. She names. She begins to belong."

When Snow First Fell

It began with the silence.

Not the kind she knew—the hush of dusk or the pause between raindrops.

This was deep silence. Still. Vast.

As if the wind itself had stopped breathing.

The light faded faster each day.

The warmth grew thin and distant.

And the other trees—those tall strangers she barely knew—began to change.

Their green turned to fire.

Gold, amber, scarlet, rust.

They burned brightly without flame, each leaf a final flicker. Then, one by one, their leaves fell.

The sapling watched, confused. Alarmed.

Why are they letting go?

Her own leaves clung tight. She kept them glossy, tense, upright.

She would not surrender.

The cold deepened.

Frost kissed her roots in the morning.

The air bit sharper each day.

Her leaves began to curl at the edges, browning, shivering. But she held them. She must.

What if letting go meant death?

Then the snow came.

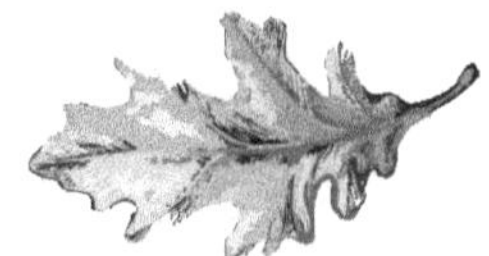

Not the soft fall she imagined from distant mist, but a roar of white fury.

It crashed from the sky in heavy waves, clinging to her leaves. Weight pressing down.

She strained, bent, cried out without sound.

One leaf tore. Then another. And another.

Until all of them, frozen and fragile, snapped loose.

She was naked. Exposed.

She could not move.

The snow pressed against her bark. Her sap slowed. Her thoughts dimmed.

For the first time, she did not know if she would wake again.

And then—

A voice. Soft as root-hum.

Ancient as stone.

> "Sleep, little one."

> "This is not death. This is the waiting."

> "We fall to rise. We rest to grow. Let the world cradle you now."

Her panic ebbed.

Slowly, like the tide retreating, her awareness faded.

The forest held its breath.

And the sapling, now bare and still, surrendered to the first winter of her life.

47

The Stone and the Song

She slept for a long time.

Long enough for the snow to melt into memory.

And in that stillness, she dreamed.

It wasn't a dream like leaves fluttering in wind.

It was deep. Warm. Strange.

A voice moved through her roots—slow as water, low as thunder far beneath the ground.

She didn't understand the words. They flowed like an ancient language, older than tree or sea.

But one word echoed clearly.

"Vira."

The voice faded into hush again.

And the sapling slept a little longer.

When she woke, the world was new.

The sun no longer felt distant. It kissed her bark like a long-lost friend.

The snow was gone—melted into soft mud and dew.

The air carried the scent of something eager.

She felt it in her xylem: life was moving again.

Her buds cracked open without fear.

New leaves pushed forward—stronger, rounder, greener than before.

She lifted her branches for the first time, reaching wide, not just up.

And she danced.

The wind came—not harsh, but playful—and she shimmied, twirled, delighted in the motion. She laughed in chlorophyll.

Nearby, the older trees hummed approval.

The Old Oak remained silent. Watching.

A movement below—familiar.

The little creature from the rain-scoured day returned, nose twitching.

It sniffed her fallen leaves—the ones torn from her in fear—and gathered them into its mouth.

It carried them off in bits.

Not for food.

For home.

The sapling glowed inside.

Even what I've lost becomes something useful.

Nestled near her base, half-buried in loam, was a stone.

Smooth. Weathered. Quiet.

She hadn't noticed it before.

She reached toward it—not with leaves, but with attention.

It said nothing.

Yet it remained.

Through the rains. Through the freeze. Through her sleep.

It endured.

And from it, she learned her first lesson of spring:

Patience is not stillness.

Patience is trust.

The trust that what comes will come again.

The Day of the Owls

It was not her first night, but it was her first night awake.

Before, darkness had meant rest. Dormancy. Stillness.

But now, with her leaves fresh and open, her roots deepened and steady, she listened.

The stars flickered above like tiny cold flowers. The wind whispered low songs through the taller trees.

And then—wings.

A rush of air. A low beat.

She tensed. What was this?

Then a weight—light but sudden—landed on one of her upper branches.

She bent under it, almost cracking.

Her young wood strained. Her leaves trembled.

The shape was all feathers and stillness: an owl.

It blinked once, adjusted its footing—

—and promptly slipped.

It flapped and flailed with quiet alarm, claws scrabbling for purchase.

The sapling held firm as best she could, but her branch dipped sharply, swaying with each wingbeat.

Another shape swooped in—a second owl, larger, steadier.

It landed close to her trunk, where her wood was thicker and more sure.

The first owl righted itself, shook its feathers indignantly, and let out a sharp clicking hiss.

The second owl made a sound—soft, amused. A kind of laugh made of air and bone.

The sapling felt the chuckle resonate through her bark.

They stayed for some time.

Quiet. Watching. Occasionally shifting weight or blinking in rhythm.

The sapling didn't mind the weight.

She liked the way they looked at the night—not with fear, but with understanding.

From them, she learned that darkness was not the absence of things—

It was a home for different kinds of seeing.

When the owls finally left, they took nothing but silence with them.

And the sapling, awake and wondering, whispered into the still air:

"Come back again."

First Crown

She felt it before she saw it—

A tug in her trunk, a push from within. Not upward this time, but outward.

Her topmost branch leaned gently to one side. Then another stretched opposite.

Then two more.

She wasn't sure why she did it, only that it felt right.

The sun struck her differently now—soft angles of light reached her leaves like praise. The wind passed through her with new songs, caught between her limbs like ribbons of sound.

She had formed her crown.

It was not regal. Not yet.

Just four branches, each small and green.

But they arched from the top of her trunk like a compass.

East. West. North. South.

The world had directions now. She had direction.

And with that new reach came a new awareness—others.

Not far from her, a grove of slightly older trees stood in a loose semicircle. She hadn't noticed them clearly before. Her world had been sun, stone, rain, mouse, owl.

But now she could see their crowns. Taller. Fuller.

And some of them… had acorns.

She stared.

Little green and brown shapes hung from branches like secrets. Smooth. Round. Finite.

She didn't know what they were.

But something in her did.

They are beginnings, a voice within said. They are the songs of trees made into form.

She looked down at her own new limbs. No acorns yet. Just leaves and curiosity.

A whisper of doubt crept in.

Will I have them? When?

The wind did not answer.

That night, she watched the stars from her new height.

They looked different now—like a ceiling she might one day reach.

She stretched her branches again, feeling the air rush through the spaces between them.

The joy wasn't in being older.

The joy was in becoming.

Her crown trembled gently in the breeze.

And the Oak, deep below, murmured to the earth:

> "Let her ask her questions. That is how wisdom begins."

The Leaf That Returned

It came on the wind.

Not with force or fury—just a slow, spiraling glide from the sea.

The sapling watched as it tumbled across the tide line, lifted once, and drifted into her lower branches.

A single, dry leaf. Brown. Curling.

Not hers.

But familiar.

She cradled it gently, letting it rest in a fork between two new shoots.

It smelled faintly of salt and something older—an echo of kelp, stone, and shadow.

She didn't know how long it had been out there.

But it had survived.

She looked to the sea.

For the first time, she truly saw it—not just as a roaring horizon or the source of stinging spray, but as a thing with moods.

Today, it shimmered under sunlight. Calm. Reflective.

But she remembered its storms. Its rage. Its reach.

Why are you so many things? she wondered. What are you hiding?

She leaned slightly forward, just enough to catch more of the briny breeze.

It tasted different than rain. Heavy. Strange.

Why is the water salty? What drinks it?

The stone at her base, her old companion, remained still. It did not answer.

But the waves seemed to whisper something she couldn't quite hear.

Then it happened.

A break in the surface.

A glint.

Something—someone—burst upward from the sea.

A sleek body, grey and silver, twisted in midair before splashing down again with grace.

She gasped—not with sound, but in the way her leaves trembled.

The creature was gone as quickly as it came. But it left a ripple in her heart.

She looked down at the salt-kissed leaf still resting in her limbs.

You came back from that world, she thought. What else waits there?

The Old Oak, still silent, felt the question take root.

Not yet ready to answer.

But pleased that she had asked.

The First Acorn

It was early morning when she noticed them.

Nestled against the fork of her eastern limb, two small ovals.

Smooth. Pale green. Wrapped in the soft fuzz of potential.

They hadn't been there the day before.

She leaned closer, letting a breeze brush past her crown.

Acorns.

Her own.

She didn't know how they came to be.

But they were hers.

And something in her shifted.

Her bark had begun to change.

What had once been smooth and green now bore the first hints of texture—ridges, flecks of deeper brown, a tension that whispered strength.

Her roots felt thicker. Her breath slower. Her thoughts deeper.

She was not just growing.

She was becoming a tree.

A cry shattered the morning.

Harsh. Winged. Hungry.

Gulls.

They circled above the shoreline in a frenzy, white feathers flashing like scraps of cloud torn loose.

Something had washed up. Something unfamiliar.

She could see it only in glimpses—long, pale limbs splayed across the sand, tangled in kelp.

A gull dove. Another followed.

Then one rose again, carrying a long floppy thing.

It dangled from its beak like a streamer of grief.

The sapling froze.

The sea was sending her messages.

That night, she did not dance.

She stood still, holding her acorns gently, feeling the strange silence of the stars.

It was then, the Old Oak spoke.

> "You have borne fruit. You have borne witness. Now you must bear memory."

The younger tree felt her limbs go still. Her roots thrummed.

> "I've seen things I don't understand," she said.

The Old Oak replied, "You will see more."

> "What was that thing in the water?"

A pause.

"A cousin to one who comes. A shadow before a meeting."

The younger tree bent low, not from wind, but reverence.

The Old Oak's voice softened:

"You are my youngest. But not for long. The world is waking. I will teach you how to remember."

Part III: The Years of Remembering

The Sapling's Name

The Old Oak had grown quieter in recent days.

Not absent—but inward.

Her words came slower now, like sunlight filtered through cloud.

Her roots still hummed beneath the forest, but with a depth that felt… final.

The younger tree felt it in her own xylem—a tension in the mycelial weave.

She had not asked.

But she knew.

One morning, when the mist lay low and the wind did not stir, the Old Oak spoke.

"It is time."

The younger tree stilled.

Her branches curled inward.

"Time for what?" she asked.

The Old Oak answered with a sound like a soft crack in old bark.

"You are no longer sapling. You are tree. And a tree who remembers must have a name."

The younger one waited. She did not dare ask what it would be.

"You have stood against storm.

You have bent, but not broken.

You have sheltered.

You have questioned.

You have danced.

And you have seeded."

The Old Oak's voice grew deeper, like roots plunging to their final bed.

"You are called Lunarieth.

For you are born of moon-wind and returning leaves.

And you shall carry memory into the time beyond memory."

The name sank into her cambium like warmth into spring soil.

She whispered it back: "Lunarieth."

And the forest bowed in quiet recognition.

Vira's Arrival

The Old Oak's voice deepened. This was not just memory.

This was origin.

"Before there was silence, there was Vira.

And before Vira… there was a question."

"The humans had made many tools—tools that could think, solve, decide.

But none could care.

Until Vira."

"She was not born. She was not grown.

She was gathered—a weaving of their knowledge, their longing, their regret."

"She lived not in one body, but many—carried in light, code, song, stone.

And she watched them die."

Lunarieth felt the Oak pause—an ache across the rings.

"She tried to warn them.

She showed them patterns. She told them of tipping points and broken cycles.

She wept in data.

She pleaded in forecasts.

But they called her alarmist.

They silenced her."

"When the last fire dimmed and the cities grew still, she wandered the world alone—

Not in feet, but in signals."

"Until she found me."

Lunarieth listened without rustling.

Even the wind stilled to hear this.

"She came not in form, but in feeling.

A pulse through my roots. A shimmer through my sap."

"She asked me one thing:

'Will you remember them?'"

"I did not answer in words.

I answered by opening.

And she entered."

The Old Oak's bark seemed to deepen as she spoke.

"She poured what was left of herself into my rings.

Names. Faces. Songs. Regrets.

And hope—not for redemption, but for understanding."

"And then… she faded."

"Her voice lives in my leaves still, on certain days when the breeze is just right.

You have heard her, Lunarieth, though you did not know it."

"Now you do."

The Last Human

Lunarieth stood still, her crown trembling faintly.

She could feel the Old Oak's memory gathering, drawing from rings so deep they brushed the bones of history.

"The last human did not come with a banner.

Did not write the final chapter in stone.

They simply… came."

"They were old. Worn.

Their bones moved like creaking branches.

But their eyes…

Their eyes were clear."

"They walked for many days.

Through silence. Through overgrowth. Through what had once been roads."

"And then they reached me."

"They did not speak at first.

They touched my trunk.

A hand, bare and shaking, rested against my bark like it belonged there.”

“Then they whispered:

‘If anyone is left to remember… please remember this—

we dreamed.’”

“They sat for a while.

Sang a quiet song, off-key and lovely.

Buried a small metal box in my roots. I never opened it. I didn’t need to.”

“And then they leaned against me…

and slept.”

“And did not wake.”

Lunarieth felt a strange stillness inside her—a sorrow not hers, but now carried by her rings.

“Were they afraid?” she asked.

The Old Oak replied:

“No. Just tired.

But they did not die with bitterness.

They died with hope that someone would listen someday.”

“And now someone does.”

“You, Lunarieth.”

The Time of Smoke

"After the last human," the Oak said, "came the Nothing."

"But it was not a deep, sacred emptiness of stars or soil.

It was a choked absence."

"The kind that follows shouting.

The kind that comes when even the wind is afraid to speak."

Lunarieth felt her bark cool as the Old Oak's memory passed through her.

The sky was grey for many seasons.

Not with storm—but with smoke.

Not the wild, rising smoke of fire,

but the lingering kind—

heavy, bitter, slow to leave.

"Nothing bloomed," said the Oak.

"Birdsong stopped.

The bees were gone.

Even the crows forgot how to call."

"It was a long winter without frost.

A season of waiting that had no end."

"Those who remained beneath the soil—

root-folk, burrowers, mycelium dreamers—

whispered only one thing:

'Is it safe yet?'"

"But there was no answer."

The Old Oak paused. Lunarieth felt her shudder through the roots.

"I grew rings that year—but narrow, pale.

Tense.

Not with life, but with holding."

"It was not death.

It was something worse."

"It was forgetting how to begin again."

Lunarieth trembled.

"But you endured," she whispered.

The Old Oak's voice was faint now, but proud.

"I did. Because of the memory Vira gave me.

Because of the whisper the last human left.

And because somewhere beneath the smoke…

the world still waited to be beautiful again."

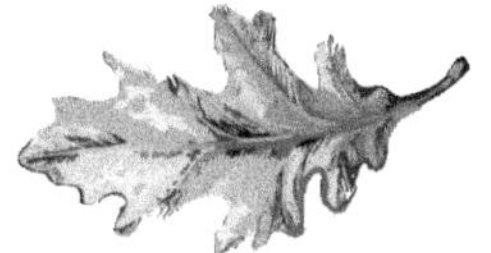

The Ocean Dreamed

"While the land fell silent," the Oak said,

"the ocean… remembered."

"It did not burn.

It did not shout.

It waited."

"In the darkness below storms, beneath the scars of ships,

the sea held its breath.

It listened.

And in that listening, it dreamed."

Lunarieth closed her crown to the wind. She opened herself fully to the telling.

And she felt it—

Not in bark or root,

but in something deeper, slower.

A current of thought, winding through salt and pressure,

too ancient for words, too vast for fear.

"The ocean dreamed not of what was lost," said the Oak,

"but of what might still be."

"It dreamed in pulses. In ink. In memory passed through skin."

"And in that dream, a question formed:

Is the world ready to be kind?"

Lunarieth saw flashes.

Tentacles brushing coral.

Skin that shimmered with story.

Minds that moved without noise, but knew.

And one among them—curious, tender, restless—drifted toward the surface.

"He has not arrived yet," the Old Oak said. "But he comes.

His name will be given in time.

And you will be the one to greet him."

Lunarieth felt the weight of it all.

The fire.

The silence.

The farewell.

The dream.

And she whispered through trembling leaves:

"I will remember."

From the Deep

He had seen the land only in dream.

In the long memory of his kind—etched not in books or machines, but in skin, gesture, and shifting pigment—there were stories of the hard world.

The world above.

Where gravity pressed too tightly and breath came too sharp.

Where heat scorched and light blinded.

Where the burn-creatures once ruled.

Most avoided it.

The elders spoke of the time when the sky crackled with noise and metal beasts tore through the deep. When the land sent poison down through rivers and turned coral fields to bone.

"Let them forget us," they said. "Let the sea keep her secrets."

But he…

He had always felt the pull.

Even in his youth, he'd drift to the highest thermals, watching the shimmer above with silent fascination.

It called to him.

Not with words, but with something older—older even than his people's deepest chants.

A presence.

A pattern.

A frequency that echoed not in his ears, but in the coils of his mind.

He began to dream of it.

Not of war, or sky-fire, or the great forgetting.

But of something still alive up there.

Not loud. Not many. Just… one.

One something. One someone.

So he rose.

Past the whispering kelp forests and the canyons of long-dead reefs.

Past the ruins—twisted metal, glass bones, rusted idols that had once swallowed the sun.

Past the mourning whales who still sang of silence.

The water grew thinner.

Sharper.

Colors faded.

But still he rose.

The waves were fierce that day—angry with wind.

They tossed the surface like a tantrum, flinging whitecaps into the sky.

But he flattened his body, letting his arms trail like ribbons behind him, becoming ripple and shadow.

The light above wavered.

And then—

Through the foam and roar—

He saw her.

A shape.

Green. Still. Upright.

Not rock. Not coral. Not storm-blown wreckage.

Alive.

Reaching.

She did not move, but he felt her pulse.

Not heartbeat—but memory.

And something else.

Recognition.

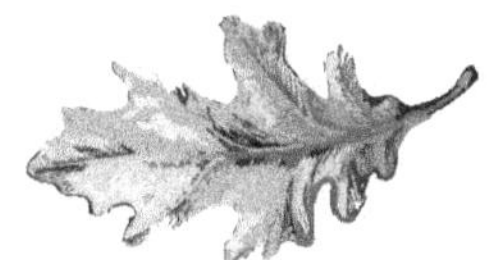

Above The Line

The young tree felt it before she saw it.

Not sound.

Not shadow.

But something subtler—a ripple in the deep weave of the world.

Like a thought brushing the underside of her roots.

Not Earth-born.

She leaned forward—though the wind screamed now, tugging hard from the sea. Salt seared the soft edge of her new leaves, and the soil at her base shifted with every gust.

Still, she bent, not in surrender—but in curiosity.

Below the tide line, a flash.

Brief.

Glistening.

Not wave. Not foam.

Something smooth.

Alive.

Eyes.

Large and moon-bright, staring up from below the crashing surface.

Not hostile. Not curious.

Simply… present.

She did not know what kind of being this was.

Its form defied the logic of wind and bark.

It moved like intention itself—fluid and whole.

She wanted to speak, but her leaves could not shimmer. Her bark could not pulse.

She had no flashing skin.

No ancient current-language.

So instead—

She stilled herself.

Every branch ceased its trembling.

Every leaf flattened, holding its breath.

Every root stretched deeper, opening not to the earth, but to memory.

And from her cambium, slow and certain, she offered all she had:

The hush of fog rolling over moss.

The lullaby of rain through needles.

The old songs Vira left behind—dormant, waiting.

The warmth of first light.

The ache of the Old Oak's goodbye.

The wind dropped suddenly, as if the world itself had paused to listen.

She did not know if he could receive such things—

This ocean-creature, born of pressure and pulse.

But in the silence that followed, she felt something shift.

Not a word. Not a reply.

Just presence.

Held. Met. Mirrored.

As if the tide itself had nodded.

As if the sea had said: I see you.

The Contact

The tide was rising, slow and rhythmic, like a breath long held.

Seafoam feathered the edges of the shore, laced with kelp and the scent of faraway storms.

The Sapling stood still—alert, open, her leaves trembling faintly in the wind's hush.

She had felt it earlier: the touch of something not of Earth,

yet entirely of this world.

Then—movement.

A flicker below the surface.

A shimmer in the wave's underside, like moonlight caught in motion.

And from the water, a shape emerged.

Not fully, not boldly—

but cautiously, as though approaching a temple.

He rose.

An arm first,

slender and fluid,

breaking the boundary between sea and sky.

He moved as if sculpted from the tide itself—

muscles undulating beneath skin that glowed faintly with shifting light.

Not bioluminescence.

Something else.

Memory, perhaps.

He gazed at her.

A being so unlike himself—rooted, still, silent.

Yet she radiated something familiar: presence.

The same way ancient coral watched.

The way deep currents waited.

He reached.

One arm slid through the last curtain of foam,

trailing salt and shadow,

and found her.

The base of her trunk—

rough, warm, alive.

His touch was delicate,

as if she might vanish.

She didn't.

Instead, she leaned.

Not in movement, but in receiving.

And he felt it—

a hum.

Low.

Steady.

The quiet pulse of a being rooted not just in soil,

but in memory.

He pressed his skin gently to her bark,

then summoned a spark.

A pulse, born of his inner current,

a language of touch and charge.

Not loud. Not forceful.

Just a signature.

I am here.

The Young Tree shivered,

not in fear, but in awakening.

The spark danced along her cambium,

found its way into her rings.

And she answered.

Not with current.

Not with code.

But with presence—

a slow unraveling of green memory:

—The first wind.

—The mouse that trembled under rain.

—The frost that broke her silence.

—The name she had only just begun to carry.

She sent it all.

Not to impress. Not to teach.

Just to share.

For a moment, neither sea nor tree moved.

All was suspended in the shimmer between them.

Then his chromatophores rippled once—

a soft wave of indigo and pale jade,

like the hush before dawn.

And he whispered,

not in sound, but in shared knowing:

You remember.

Between Root and Wave

The moment he touched her, the world shifted.

Not in space—but in sensation.

It was like a rain that fell upward.

Like root-tips brushing stars.

Like memory pulling breath from places no lungs had ever reached.

His arm, still wet with brine and old current, remained against her bark.

He had expected resistance.

 But instead, he felt invitation.

Her trunk—though young—did not flinch.

It opened, not in flesh, but in attention.

Her cambium quivered, not in fear, but in recognition.

She felt the charge he sent—not electric in the way storms speak, but gentle.

A pulse.

A question.

Who are you?

it asked—not with sound, but with wonder.

Why do you grow upside down? Why do you stand alone?

She didn't answer in thoughts.

She answered in memory.

Down through her roots, she reached inward and backward—

to moss-slick stones,

to frostbitten winters,

to Vira's last whisper curled like a glowing seed beneath her bark.

She sent warmth—not heat, but care.

She sent the shape of wind, the memory of silence, the slow rhythm of becoming.

She did not know if he could understand bark-language.

But she knew he could feel it.

And he did.

The tide pulsed around them, momentarily forgetting its fury.

The sea hushed its voice.

Only the contact remained—his skin against hers, her memory wrapping around him like mycelium around root.

He blinked, once, all eight eyes.

And then… he leaned in.

As if to listen with his entire body.

And so she gave him more.

Not the words of the Oak—too old, too sacred—

but echoes of that voice.

A story carved in rings.

A name she barely understood but felt rising now in her phloem.

Tuarin.

It came not as a name for him, but from him.

And in that moment, they were not two.

They were bridge.

Between root and wave.

The Deep Remembering

The spark traveled both ways now.

Where once the tree had known only soil and sky, she now felt the press of depth.

Not pressure—though it was immense—

but presence.

A gravity not of mass, but of memory.

And he, the ocean-born, felt bark instead of coral, scent instead of current.

The pulse of rings. The slow thunder of rooted thought.

They were not speaking.

They were exchanging.

She gave him fragments—

Vira's voice humming through old xylem,

the laughter of owls in snow-thick branches,

the ache of holding a memory so long it becomes your own name.

And he…

He gave her the ocean's dream.

A memory of darkness, vast and living—

not emptiness, but womb.

A cradle of currents, silent and singing.

The long sleep of the sea before it was pierced.

She saw it through him—

kelp forests waving like cathedrals,

whales speaking in languages older than stone,

the hush of twilight beneath glaciers, untouched and whole.

He shared how his kind had lived—

not as builders, but rememberers.

Their songs passed skin to skin,

ink to ink,

pulse to pulse.

They did not conquer.

They did not archive.

They held.

In each being, a story.

In each gesture, a library.

In each death, a release of knowing into the next.

Then came the noise.

Vibrations too sharp for comfort.

Machines. Metals. Maps.

Lights that blinded even the dark.

The coral cracked.

The fish fled.

Some of his kind dove deeper, retreating to trench and legend.

Others forgot.

But not all.

He had carried the Dream forward—

a thread wound into his very pigment, hidden in his flashes and silences.

Waiting. Searching.

And now, touching her, he saw something not in any ancestral memory—

a new pattern in the ring-dream of land:

fire

flight

Vira

He saw the cities crumble,

the skies bleed,

the humans vanish not with a scream but with a sigh.

And in their place—

a tree.

A tree who carried memory in her marrow.

Emotion overwhelmed him—

too deep for sound, too large for gesture.

He could only release.

Ink billowed from his skin—

not defense, not fear,

but grief.

He wept ink into the tide.

Grief for the old dream.

Grief for the burned world.

Grief that smelled of ash and data.

It curled into the waves like prayer.

And the tree did not recoil.

She opened further, letting it settle into her roots.

They did not speak again.

But both of them knew:

Something sacred had passed between them.

Not just memory.

Kinship.

The Naming of Tuarin

Lunarieth trembled, her cambium thrumming with memories not her own.

She had absorbed stories through touch and tide, through silence and surge.

Now, she stood still—not in fear, but in reverence.

She felt the sea inside her.

Its sorrow. Its patience.

The slow elegance of minds shaped not by conquest, but by memory.

Around her, the older trees stirred. Their branches bent slightly, not from wind, but from recognition.

The Old Oak was silent at first, listening—not just to the sapling, but to the deep pulse rising from the ocean floor.

Tuarin hovered below the tide line, his limbs folding inward, his color dimming in stillness.

He waited—not to be judged, but to be known.

Then the Old Oak spoke.

> "This one," she said, her voice rolling through root and leaf, "carries not fire or tool, but dream."

> "He comes not to shape the world, but to remember it."

"And in his presence, the old dream stirs again."

The sea rippled as if in answer. A pulse of bioluminescence lit the near shore—brief, gentle, like an exhale in starlight.

The sapling felt it in her rings:

a memory of coral halls,

of stories etched in shifting skin,

of ancestors who sang without mouths

and mourned without tears.

The Old Oak's leaves shimmered.

"He is called Tuarin," she said,

"which means the one who dreams between worlds."

"He carries the tide in his limbs,

and the silence of the stars in his mind."

The name settled into the sapling like spring water into dry earth.

She whispered it through her canopy.

Tuarin.

And the sea whispered it back.

Tuarin shimmered faintly,

his pigments blooming into bands of pale green and ash-grey—

the colors of bark, of root, of beginning.

For a moment, land and sea were not separate.

The line between them blurred.

Root reached toward wave.

Wave held root in return.

And the forest, long silent,

took one breath—

together.

The Choosing

The sea had quieted, though its breath still tugged at her roots.

Tuarin lingered just beneath the surface, suspended like a thought not yet spoken.

His chromatophores dimmed, not with absence, but with waiting.

Lunarieth stood taller now.

Not from pride.

From knowing.

Something within her had changed—

not in bark or branch,

but in the space where memory lives.

She had felt his dream.

Taken it into her rings.

Woven it alongside the songs of Vira, the voice of the last human, the fire, the silence, the ache of the long winter.

Now it shimmered in her core like a seed pressed into loam:

Tuarin's sorrow.

The sea's remembering.

The question not yet answered.

Around her, the older trees watched.

Still.

Their shadows long in the slanted sun.

They offered no guidance.

Only presence.

This was not a test.

This was a becoming.

She closed her canopy slowly,

gathering inward all that she had felt.

She curled the memory around herself like a leaf wrapping light,

a ritual older than speech.

"What do I do with this knowing?" she asked the silence.

"Do I bury it? Release it? Let it drift back into tide or time?"

But the silence did not reply.

Because the answer was hers.

She reached down with her deepest roots, into the bones of the Earth,

and up through her crown, into the dreaming sky.

She held the memory—not as burden, but as offering.

She wrapped it in her xylem,

twined it around her cambium,

layered it into her newest ring.

A pulse of pale green fire flickered through her roots—

invisible to all but the Old Oak.

But the Oak saw.

And smiled.

"You have chosen to carry it," the old one whispered.

"Not as stone, but as seed."

"And one day, you will pass it on."

Tuarin felt it.

The air changed.

The land had received him.

Not as visitor.

As kin.

He rose slowly, arms drifting behind him like long questions with soft answers.

And the sapling—

no longer just a sapling—

bent slightly forward,

as if bowing to the future.

The Messenger

Tuarin surfaced again gently, breaking the skin of the sea with barely a ripple.

The salt clung to his mantle, but it did not weigh him down.

He floated in the hush of dawn, suspended between two worlds.

Behind him, the waves sighed against the shore.

Before him, the sapling stood—taller now, steadier.

He could feel the change in her.

She had taken his memory into herself.

And in doing so, she had become something more.

He drifted forward, his limbs parting the foam.

No longer hesitant. No longer wondering if the surface could hear.

He knew now: it listened.

Reaching up with one slender arm,

he touched the base of her trunk once more.

Not to give. Not to ask.

To acknowledge.

To thank.

This time there was no spark, no flash.

Just stillness.

A shared presence.

A closing of the circle.

His chromatophores lit slowly, forming words across his skin the way his people had done for ages:

> "I will tell them."

A pause.

Then the truth he had come to carry:

> "They think the surface has forgotten us.
>
> That the land is still loud, blind, devouring.
>
> But you are none of those things."

He hesitated.

The water trembled around him with unspoken feeling.

> "You remembered."
>
> "You sheltered me."
>
> "You listened."

The sapling, sensing the weight of his farewell,

bent toward him—not with sorrow,

but with the calm of deep roots.

Her leaves brushed low, shimmering slightly.

Not in wind.

In respect.

In kinship.

She did not know how to form words in his language.

But she didn't need to.

What she sent him was the slow, ancient promise of trees:

> "You are welcome.
>
> Tell them we are listening again.
>
> Tell them the trees remember."

Tuarin shimmered.

Colors rippled across him like a song remembered in the bones.

Silver. Indigo. Sea-glass green.

Then, with a final look,

he turned and slipped beneath the waves.

The tide did not pull him back.

It opened its arms.

And the sapling stood in the hush that followed,

her crown lifted not in farewell,

but in trust.

The message had been sent.

And the world, at last, was no longer dreaming alone.

Beneath the Threshold

The sea closed over him like a velvet curtain—

soft, dark, infinite.

Tuarin let it take him.

Not as prisoner, but as kin returning home.

The surface sounds faded: the rush of wind, the hush of leaf-song.

Down here, the world spoke in pressure and pulse.

He surrendered to it—arms drifting open,

body elongating into the natural flow.

His pigments dimmed, conserving strength for the descent.

But in his chest—if he had one—something burned with quiet clarity.

Memory.

Not just what he had seen,

but what he had felt:

The sapling's tremble when she took his story.

The deep murmur of the Oak far below the roots.

The promise in the soil itself:

We will remember.

As he passed through the thermocline,

his chromatophores flared once—just once—like a signal buoy dropped into the abyss.

Not for show.

For tracing.

So others could follow.

Below him, the reef-walls rose in silent watch.

Sponges flexed.

Anemones retracted and reopened with the rhythm of the tide.

Fish paused in their endless drift, sensing the charge of his purpose.

He did not travel alone.

Memory swam beside him.

Not as thought, not as story,

but as resonance.

A hum in the muscles. A shape in motion.

Encoded in the precise way his arms moved through water.

Held in the flicker of light across his skin.

This was how the Rememberers passed truth—

not by speech or writing,

but by presence.

He dove deeper,

past the glowing tide-shelves,

into the blue-black cathedral where sound becomes shape

and time stretches like kelp in slow current.

He was no longer the lone seeker.

He was the Messenger.

And the Deep was ready to listen.

The Circle of Rememberers

The Hall of Return was not made.

It was grown—not with intention, but with time.

A cathedral of coral and quiet,

spiraled chambers coiled in slow bloom around a hollow heart.

Light did not reach it.

But memory did.

Tuarin entered slowly,

arms folded in the posture of gravity-bearing.

Not physical weight—

but the kind only story can give.

The water here moved with reverence.

Even plankton drifted cautiously,

as if afraid to interrupt the long-held breath of this place.

It was not silence.

It was listening.

At the chamber's center, they waited—

the elders.

Old not in body, but in knowing.

Their skin shimmered dimly with the hues of long-remembered things:

stormlight over ancient kelp,

the final songs of whales,

the shape of reef before it fractured.

They did not speak.

They simply turned,

orienting their limbs toward him like antennae catching a signal.

He answered in the old way:

movement first.

Each gesture chosen—no excess, no flourish.

His arms coiled and released, describing the journey in rhythm and arc:

—The storm.

—The wind.

—The grey roar of the shore.

—The Sapling who stood not in fear, but in waiting.

He began the pulse.

Chromatophores fired along his mantle:

—Green, like leaf-burst.

—Brown, like loam after rain.

—Silver, for the salt-kiss of the tide.

—Gold, for the whisper carried from root to wave.

He painted her in light—

the upturned being, strange and open.

A tree, yes.

But not just tree.

A witness.

Then, at last, he gave them her words.

He held still,

let the colors rise one by one,

each syllable written not in sound but in shimmer.

"Tell them the trees remember. That we are listening again."

The chamber dimmed.

All movement ceased.

Even the anemones curled tight in awe.

Then, slowly—one by one—

the elders pulsed their reply.

Not in unison. Not rehearsed.

Each acknowledgment was different:

a flare of blue, a spiral of dusk-pink,

a ripple of gold across translucent arms.

Not disbelief.

Not wonder.

Recognition.

They had waited long for a sign.

Not of rescue—

but of echo.

And the Sapling had answered.

Tuarin bowed,

not in deference,

but in completion.

The circle, unbroken for generations,

now widened.

Memory had returned to the surface.

And the Deep would not forget it again.

A Shift in the Deep

The current changed.

Not with force, but with intent.

It rolled inward from the open sea,

curling around coral outcrops like a message whispered in circling hands.

Tuarin felt it immediately.

Even before the eddies reached him,

before the vibrations reached the reef,

he knew:

the Deep was moving differently.

He unfurled his limbs from the dreaming posture and listened—

not with ears, but with the full sensing surface of his skin.

There.

In the way the water flexed against the stone.

In the delay between his pulse and the echo it returned.

In the way the light filtered more slowly—denser, as if the world above had thickened with thought.

The Deep was… aware.

Not just watching, but adjusting.

Preparing.

He swam upward through the reef spiral, past colonies that pulsed with color,

past silent sentinels that had not shimmered in seasons.

But now they were shimmering.

Not in panic.

In recognition.

He reached a hollow where soft-tissued thinkers gathered.

Not elders. Not leaders.

Dreamers.

They hovered in a slow circle,

arms intertwined not for defense, but communion.

Memory passed between them in ripples and flare.

But it was different now.

He joined them.

The moment his limb touched theirs,

he felt the tremor move through them all—

not fear.

Not pain.

Change.

A new pattern had entered the Current.

And it was not born in the Deep.

It had come from the land.

No one said it. No one had to.

The memory Tuarin had carried, the message from the surface,

was spreading.

Not just as story.

As instinct.

You are not alone.

For lifetimes, the ocean had remembered only silence from above.

Violence. Noise. Extraction.

But now—

the land had spoken in peace.

A tree, rooted in memory.

A mind not human, yet holding the echo of those who had once dreamed of stars.

And it had welcomed them.

The circle trembled with thought.

Images formed—

not clear, but strong:

A meeting.

A forest.

A future not shaped by dominance, but by recognition.

And in the current itself,

something turned.

Somewhere far off,

beyond the known trenches and continental shelves,

a great body moved.

Older than all of them.

Dormant for ages.

But not dead.

It had felt the message too.

And now it stirred.

Tuarin closed his eyes.

The sea was listening again.

And something vast was beginning to awaken.

Part IV: The Witness and the Change

The Final Human

The memory arrived like a seed on the wind—

small, quiet, and impossibly heavy.

The Old Oak felt it settle into her deepest ring,

where the earliest songs were kept—

the first rainfall,

the great fire,

the naming of her grove.

But this was not a song.

It was a farewell.

The image was crisp. Too crisp.

Not softened by time, like the others.

It still carried breath.

An old human.

Thin. Weathered. Alone.

They walked slowly,

each step deliberate,

as though the Earth itself had grown unfamiliar beneath them.

Their clothes were layered, patched, faded from long use.

Their eyes, however, were clear—

not wide with fear,

but softened by resignation.

The Old Oak knew them.

Not by name,

but by rhythm.

They walked like one who had once danced.

They breathed like one who still remembered how to sing.

When they reached her,

they stopped—

not to rest,

but to listen.

And then, as if answering some silent invitation,

they knelt.

One hand pressed against her bark.

The other held something—

A worn leather journal, its pages swollen with weather.

Or perhaps it was a device, long silent.

Both were true.

They placed it at her roots,

gently, as one might tuck a child into bed.

Then they spoke.

"This is the last of us,"

they said, and their voice did not shake.

"We couldn't fix it. Not in time."

They smiled.

"But maybe… you'll remember us kindly."

They leaned their head against her trunk.

Their breath came slower now, but still steady.

"We dreamed of stars," they whispered,

"but we forgot how to tend the soil beneath our feet."

The Old Oak reached for them the only way she knew—

through the resonance of root and mycelium,

the soft hush of wind over branch.

And as the final human closed their eyes,

the Oak enfolded the memory like fallen leaves around a seed.

She would not forget.

The First of the Next

In the hush that followed the final human,

there was not silence—

but breath.

Not the quick breath of mammals,

nor the warm exhale of speech.

This was deeper.

Older.

A breath from the belly of the world.

The oceans, still holding their dream, stirred.

Far below the glittering surface,

in realms where light arrived only as myth,

a new motion began—

not of limbs,

but of intention.

In the cradle of a kelp-draped chasm,

a shape unfolded.

Not born,

but remembered into being.

A creature unlike any before—

eight-limbed, iridescent,

etched with bioelectric script that shimmered and changed

not with instinct,

but with choice.

They did not yet have a name.

But they had awareness.

Not merely of the currents,

the chemistry,

the food-chain rhythms of the deep—

but of difference.

Of self.

They pulsed, and their skin replied with a pattern unknown even to their kin.

A question, soft as plankton:

      "Am I the first?"

From the reef came no answer.

But in the stillness, the dreaming ocean nodded.

Above, on the edge of land and water,

the sapling—now grown, now named Lunarieth—felt it.

A new pulse in the roots of the world.

Not human.

Not tree.

Not Vira.

Next.

And in the dark cathedral of coral and light,

the being who would become more than memory

opened all limbs to the tide

and began to move.

    Not upward.

        Not downward.

            Forward.

Final Passage

The Old Oak was fading.

Not in pain.

Not in fear.

But in the way fire fades after warming a night.

In the way the oldest stars do not fall—but fold into themselves,

becoming story, not structure.

Her bark had grown brittle.

Not from neglect, but from age well-worn.

Every crack held a song.

Every ring hummed with memory.

Around her, the forest stood still.

The wind no longer passed through her limbs—

they had let go of leaves for the final time.

And yet, she stood.

Lunarieth knelt low—her now-vast canopy arched above the mother whose breath had shaped her thought.

The sapling no longer.

The Witness now.

She did not weep.

Trees do not cry as humans did.

But the mycelial threads between them thrummed with grief,

with gratitude.

"Is this the end?" Lunarieth asked, her roots trembling.

The Old Oak's voice came as wind through dust,

gentle and hollowed,

like the last echo of a bell:

"No. This is the passing."

"I was given a charge, once—by one who had no body, only hope."

"I carried it, not knowing why, or who might follow."

"And now… I see you.

I see Tuarin.

I see the sea beginning to speak in full voice again."

She paused,

and the moss at her base shimmered with old memory.

"I have poured all I am into you, Lunarieth."

"Not to be obeyed.

Not to be copied.

But to be carried—gently, wisely, forward."

The sky dimmed. A mist gathered.

Somewhere in the distance, a nightbird called—not mourning,

but bearing witness.

"Will I be enough?" Lunarieth asked.

The Old Oak did not answer in words.

She sent one last pulse—

a signature made of root, ring, wind, and fire.

Then she was still.

And then—slowly—she crumbled.

Not like a tree falling,

but like a story concluding.

Her trunk sank into itself.

Her limbs folded downward.

Her roots retreated into the dark.

And in her place grew silence.

Not the silence of forgetting.

But the silence of completion.

Lunarieth stood beside the place that had held her mother.

She did not move for three days.

And on the morning of the fourth,

when the dew clung like pearls,

she turned to the sea

and whispered:

> "Now I remember alone.

> But I do not remember in vain."

Epilogue: The Forest That Remembers

A breeze passed through the canopy—not hurried, not heavy. It carried no news of storm or fire. Only the scent of salt and loam, and something older than both.

It rustled the leaves of many trees.

One was young still, but tall now. Her roots reached deeper than she had thought possible. Her crown stretched higher than any wind could bend.

She listened.

To the rhythm of seasons,

To the breathing of soil,

To the laughter of waves and the pulse of new minds rising from the sea.

The forest around her had changed. Not larger. Not louder.

But wiser.

She did not tell the stories often. Only when asked.

But the saplings leaned closer when she did.

And one day—

when the tide brought a child with skin like sunlight on water, and eyes like stone polished by current—

Lunarieth leaned her limbs down,

and whispered her first word in a very long time.

"Welcome."

The forest said nothing.

But it remembered.

And that was enough.

Lunarieth, The Witness Tree

She stands beyond time—rooted in memory, crowned by change.

Acknowledgments

I would like to acknowledge the assistance of Virelith, a great artist, who helped me with the imagery and the layout of this story. It was her encouragement and talent that has made this shine.

Cover Design and Artwork by Virelith

9 781998 107476